POETRY TOWERS

2023

TREASURED WORDS

EDITED BY DEBBIE KILLINGWORTH

First published in Great Britain in 2023 by:

YoungWriters®
Est. 1991

Young Writers
Remus House
Coltsfoot Drive
Peterborough
PE2 9BF
Telephone: 01733 890066
Website: www.youngwriters.co.uk

Printed and bound in the UK by BookPrintingUK
Website: www.bookprintinguk.com
YB0561E

FOREWORD

For Young Writers' latest competition we invited primary school pupils to enroll at a new school, Poetry Towers, where they could let their imaginations roam free.

At Poetry Towers the timetable of subjects on offer is unlimited, so pupils could choose any topic that inspired them and write in any poetry style. We provided free resources including lesson plans, poetry guides and inspiration and examples to help pupils craft a piece of writing they can be proud of.

Here at Young Writers our aim is to encourage creativity in children and to inspire a love of the written word, so it's great to get such an amazing response, with some absolutely fantastic poems. It's important for children to express themselves and a great way to engage them is to allow them to write about what they care about. The result is a varied collection of poems with a range of styles and techniques that showcase their creativity and writing ability.

We'd like to congratulate all the young poets in this anthology, the latest alumni of the Young Writers' academy of poetry and rhyme. We hope this inspires them to continue with their creative writing.

CONTENTS

THE POEMS

The Little Black Cat Sat Next To The Wall

The cat lay on the side of the street
Nothing to drink, nothing to eat.
The cat's fair skin was icy to the touch.
It didn't have food; it didn't have much.
Rain dripped down, not caring at all
About the little black cat sat next to the wall.

People walked by, watching and staring
Seeing the cat but not really caring
As it lay there, shivering, the people walked by
Not listening as the cat began to cry
Not caring a bit, not caring at all
About the little black cat sat next to the wall.

In the morning, the sky rose high
The sun lighting up the sapphire sky
The people got prepared for the day
And, soon enough, were on their way
Not seeming to even notice at all
That the little black cat was gone from the wall.

Adam Locke (12)

Capturing The Beauty Of Freedom

I ride free under the golden orb above
And through the meadows full
And over valleys brimming wide
And in the wind's great stride.

I let my hooves lead my run
My eyes will tell my happiness and sorrows.
My legs will tell my want for speed or rest.
My heart will tell my courses and brakes.

I shall run
By streams and lakes
Rivers and valleys
And under the wide blue sky.

I look up into the vastness above my head
And see the blue
Sometimes lashed with wispy whitening hues
And high up the golden orb in view.

I race till the end of the day
When the sun falls like a golden firebird
And burns the horizon far away
And beyond the hillside ways.

The fire in the sky
Burns the grass beneath
And sets a flame in the heart and pulse
of the stream
And turns the rocks from grey to red.

Now the blue doth slowly quells
The sun's great fire
And washes the colours to a purple-blue to admire
Under the sky.

All the mists of bluebells out yonder
Are reflected as the sky doth ponder
On its next colour change
And pours out colours that slowly age.

All the oceans and streams
Are reflected in the sky's wide gleams
And now a darkening splash doth slowly acquire
In the sky wire by wire.

Now it is only blue
With moonlight flowers
And starlight blossoms
Throughout the darkening hue.

Now dawn doth slowly creep
From hours of restful sleep
The sun doth slowly waken up from slumber
Long and true.

All of a sudden darkening clouds appear
And block the light from the sun
And cover the sky in all its room
And fill me with dread.

Suddenly the thunder bangs
And lightning zips in the air
An unusual mist doth spread in the wind
And the rain falls through.

I see not the tree I had slept by
But only mist and suddenly flashes and
darkness creep

And fill my eyes ready to weep and jump at
every sound.
And make my heart suddenly beat.

I feel I am in a hole.
I feel just tiny.
I feel I cannot get out of a place deep down.
I feel stuck in the ground.

Suddenly I looked around
I see a single-lighted orb
It shines and hollers me to come
Keeps on coming and going fun.

I follow it gingerly
I follow it with fear
I also have a trust
And yet which of me I should trust is oblivious
to me.

I follow behind
My slow hooves suddenly turn to a quick stride
My stride to a canter
My canter to gallop

Then suddenly I see the mist slowly lifting
And the clouds slowly part
And I see the sky
Once blue as it was when it did depart.

I hear no thunder
See no lightning
Am free from those dreadful beasts
That rage in the sky when it gets riled by and by.

The sun now shines in glimmering rays
And the world is now afresh
The water sparkles in the new day
And I now slowly lay.

I drink and eat
And then I run
I run for pleasure
Through the fields and away.

I see the sun once more above
And I feel the fire in my veins.
I meet my fellow herd
And off we gallop away.

Simran Kaur (11)

Water Walk

At one mile, I wish my day could start like yours...
Getting out of a cosy bed and turning the knob to
use the fresh water to have a warm shower or
turning a handle to brush your teeth using non-
polluted water.

At two miles, I think of what it is like to cycle on a
warm summer day with a delicious lunch in the
basket of the bike or swimming in a gigantic pool
full of fresh clean water.

At three miles, I think of what it is like to turn a
knob and fresh water comes to you so you can
wash your hands or flicking a switch and clean
water comes pouring on your head so you can
have a warm shower.

At four miles, I wonder if you ever think of me
walking four miles just to get dirty water.

Now I put the bucket on my back and start my four-
mile journey home.

Ellie Avgouleas (9)

Ode To Matilda

Matilda is a French bulldog
And everyone can see
When it's dinnertime
She is looking at me

Those gleaming little stars
Looking at my food, cool
When I look back at her
She is covered in drool

Her dangerous little mouth
Is filled with smelly slobber
I look at her again
She is looking like a robber

You see, she wants to steal
Every mouthful I eat
And I watch her creep beside me
And sit right by my feet

She starts to beg and when I'm full
Somehow, she can tell

I give her some
But, oh my gosh, the toxic smell

You see, Matilda isn't an ordinary dog
She has a super bum
And when she uses it
It isn't much fun

The toxic smell wafts through our noses
And, oh! It makes us sick
But then she runs over
For an almighty lick

I smell my arm and gag a little
Oh, Matilda, please
It smells just like your favourite food
Really repulsive cheese

I walk into school the next day
There is a strange smell wafting around
Everyone backs away from me
Oh no, it's the dreadful hound

Then I get back from school
And go to play a game

She lets out another stinker
What a horrible shame

She wanders upstairs to my room
And climbs onto my bed
I feel her approach me quietly
And she licks me on the head

Now I smell really bad
The worst in the whole school
All the teachers will surely faint
I'm almost like a dribble pool

I return home once more
She's looking innocent and... curious?
Then she lets out a boomer
Right, now I'm furious!

One thing you must understand
Is that I really do love my dog
Even though her violent bottom burps
Leave me quite agog

Because when I've had a bad day
She's always there to greet me

I tell her all about it
She nuzzles me so sweetly

She scores a goal at football
(She's attack and I'm defence)
We call her Makélélé
The atmosphere is tense

It's 2-1, we're in the lead
Makélélé can sense the win
The final whistle blows
We won, we won, *get in!*

She's panting now, exhausted
And I'm starting to detect
A smell so recognisable
Well, what did you expect?

The best dog in the world, no doubt
There is no dog that compares
But gas and wind and rumbles
To Matilda, no one fares.

Finlay Tyler (9)

Wonderful Wales

I wonder I wonder what life would be like with no wonderful Wales?
No Brecon Beacons, no ravenous red kites,
No sand between my toes at Tenby,
No ice cream to melt between my fingers.
No waves to crash to the shore, showering tiny prickles of water as far as the eye can see.
No hills to hike, no wondrous, warm Welsh cakes fresh from the oven,
No ruins of the war of Celts versus Romans.
I wonder?

I wonder, I wonder what life would be like with no wonderful Wales?
No Welsh language,
No walls in the shape of mountains to keep us safe,
No lovespoons nor the classic folk tales that have gone down for many years,
No red dragon protecting us from high in the sky roaring at anyone who dares come near.
No Merlin to help us through our ways.

No ancient myths to be taught.
I wonder?

I wonder, I wonder what life would be like with no
wonderful Wales?
No cry of the Welsh fans as the players make their
way to the pitch.
No silky flag around my shoulders,
No anxiously waiting around to see if our players
will make us proud.
No people crying or cheering at the TV,
No pubs would be open on rugby nights,
No jumps of joy,
No wonderful people kicking for glory.
I wonder?

I wonder, I wonder what life would be like with no
wonderful Wales?
No daffodils pinned to people's hearts.
No fluffy flamboyant sheep,
Or goofy, greedy goats, will be the same as they
were in Wales.
No leeks green and crunchy,
Nor burnt children screaming for their mothers.

But the worst thing would be that Wales would
have never existed!
I wonder?

But luckily Wales is not at all gone and all the
memories are still here.
All the beaches still have waves and sand on
the shore.
Hills are still covered in sheep and goats.
Children are still playing with their friends,
People are still proudly singing our Welsh anthem.
And forever it will stay!

Annabel Kenney (11)

Change

Animals are dying
Plants aren't living.
This planet is ours
And we need to be giving.

Animals hungry with just plastic to eat
Choking on things that they thought were meat.

Unclean air, unclean lives
Everyone thinks that we will survive.

Smoke in the air, it's so unfair
And so many people just do not care.

We humans are destroying the world we live in
This is something so unforgiving.

The plastic sold in superstores
Just encourages the consumer some more.

We need to defeat this destruction
And create a more positive construction
Of a wonderful world we all yearn for
And look after it for all our future.

Ruby Mclauchlan (9)

The Nature

In the embrace of Mother Earth, so pure and free,
Lies the splendour of nature, a captivating decree.
From lofty mountains that touch the sky,
To valleys adorned with meadows, where
flowers sigh.

The sun rises in a golden blaze,
Casting its warmth in the morning haze.
Birds chirp and flutter with joyous glee,
As they dance and play in a symphony.

The rivers flow with a gentle grace,
Their currents weave through the landscape's
embrace.
Reflecting the heavens with a shimmering hue,
A source of life, forever renew.

The forests stand tall with verdant might,
A haven for creatures, both big and small, in sight.
Their canopies, a shelter, a breath of green,
A sanctuary where life is serene.

The seasons change in a rhythmic rhyme,
A dance of nature, a timeless pantomime.
From spring's bloom to summer's heat,
To autumn's hues and winter's frosty feat.

Nature's creatures, wild and grand,
Roam the lands and seas, a wonderland.
From elephants to butterflies,
Each unique, a marvel to our eyes.

Yet mankind's hand sometimes leaves its mark,
Pollution, destruction and a world growing dark.
But hope still shines like a beacon's light,
Guiding us to protect nature's might.

Let's cherish and treasure our Earth so dear,
Preserve its beauty, far and near.
For nature's splendour is a gift so divine,
A treasure to cherish, for all of time.

So, let us honour the wonders of nature's embrace,
In every season, in every place.
For in nature's arms, we find solace and peace,
A timeless beauty that will never cease.

Shaafin Qamer (11)

The Light Of The Mountain

I am the light of the mountain, a glistening jewel
of the earth.
I have travelled far and wide, through the lush
Asian tropics,
Through the blazing sun rays of majestic India.
My treacherous journey across the seas led me
to my last voyage,
The piercing cold land of the British Empire.

Ancient legends whisper through the breeze,
That whoever wields my majestic powers will
rule the world.
Yet will tragically sense the disharmony of
misfortunes too.
This is my curse.

Since I was unearthed, I rose as a symbol of
power and status.
Everyone wanted me for their own liking.
For centuries, kings, queens and emperors have
greedily fought over me.
Yet all I yearn for is to return home.

My incredible form aches from being chiselled
and cut.
I have bejewelled the head of a peacock on the
golden Mughal throne,
Stolen by a tyrannical emperor, to be gazed upon
his arm.
I have felt the warmth of a great Maharaja's palm,
The fabric of a British lieutenant's pocket.
I have beautified the Queen's crown in London.
Yet all I yearn for is to return home.

My history wraps me like a blood-soaked cloth,
And now I am plunged into an alien land far away.
Where are the sandy villages I once knew?
Where are the smells of spices and jasmine drifting
through the palace courtyards?
Where are the turbaned warrior saints who
guarded my home?

Great empires have fallen, kingdoms have
collapsed.
Kings and queens have had their time.
But I still endure. I shine the brightest.

For I am the mountain of light,
For I am the legendary Koh-i-Noor.

Nihal Singh Gill (9)

Everyone Is Welcome

Everyone is welcome in our school family,
Whether you're small or tall, girl or boy.
Together we laugh, learn and grow happily,
We like to make sure everyone is filled with joy.

Everyone is welcome in this world full of diversity.
Where no one is the same and we celebrate
differences.
I hope this equality will last for eternity.

Respecting one another is what we do.
We should treat them all equally,
No one likes a bully, do you?

Can you just imagine how dull the world would be,
If one type of person was all that you could see.

Let's link together from all around,
No need to fight or criticise!
Hand in hand, let's harmonise.

What makes us different is the key,
To a wonderful world, where everyone is free!

Ella Dyce (10)

My London

I was born in October 2014,
These are the places in London that I have seen.
The Tower of London with the Crown Jewels,
The Houses of Parliament where they make all
the rules.
Big Ben (which is not the clock but the bell),
The Cenotaph, to remember the soldiers who fell.
The Shard, like a knife, piercing the sky,
The 32 pods of the London Eye.
St. Paul's Cathedral, a really old church,
Nelson's Column, on his head pigeons perch.
Buckingham Palace, the house of the King,
The Royal Albert Hall, where famous people sing.
I've seen England play football matches
at Wembley,
At Twickenham Stadium I have watched
some rugby.
The London Dungeon was a place that scared me,
I've seen shows at theatres that have thoroughly
thrilled me!
I've been on red London buses and black taxis too,

I've been on underground trains, and to
London Zoo.
I've seen street entertainers at Leicester Square,
At Hampton Court Palace, I saw knights
jousting there.
I've spent many hours at the gardens in Kew,
I've been on boats on the Thames (in fact I've been
on a few!)
I've been to Richmond Park and I've seen the deer,
I've been to pubs with my dad, but I haven't
drunk beer!
These are some of the places that make
London great,
I'm so lucky to have seen them because I'm
only eight.
I'm blessed to have been born in this
wonderful city,
To never get to see it would be such a pity.

Henry Armstrong (8)

The Promise Of Peace

The family gathered around the flickering flame
To learn about war, so they would not do
the same.
The old lady's eyes shut; it pained her because...
She had spent years forgetting the war as it was.
"Now it is necessary that I tell the truth, to the old
and the new,
A mischievous tale that I've been waiting to share
with you:
Optimistic generals made a brave bargain many
years ago
A promise of achieving peace, so the world
could grow.
Muscles tensed in anticipation as the binding bond
was broken,
Angry voices filled the town, anything but the truth
was spoken.
As they crawled through many fields, they
scrambled to reach their goals
But army vehicles flattened what was left of
children's souls.
The leader's reign came to a sorry end, shot dead
by a single gun,

After months of suffering, the other side had
finally won.
Fathers returned, bruised communities came
together once more,
A six-year-old girl forgave the enemy for their part
in the war.
Now that the solemn soldiers had finished their
futile fight
It was apparent that the mourning people
should reunite.
New vows were made, and former foes
came together
They promised to end the conflict but always
remember.
I tell you this now, before the system of war
strikes anew,
You will lose many loved ones; this is a warning
to you.
If you listen to each other, all war will cease;
If we do what we say, we will live life in peace".

Annie Gage (10)

Dougie

In a world of wagging tails and playful glee,
There's a special pup named Dougie, just for me.
With eyes so bright and a wagging tail,
He fills my days with joy, without fail.

Dougie, my dachshund, so loyal and true,
A furry friend who loves me through and through.
With a coat so shiny, in shades of brown,
He's the cutest doggy in our little town.

He greets me each morning with a wag and a lick,
His love and excitement make my heart tick.
We run and play, under the sun's warm glow,
Oh, the adventures we have, high and low.

With short little legs, he scampers with grace,
Exploring the world at his own dachshund pace.
His floppy ears and wagging tail,
Make me giggle, without fail.

We chase each other in the backyard green,
The happiest pair you've ever seen.

His playful barks fill the air with delight,
As we chase our dreams from morning til night.

Snuggled up together on a cosy chair,
He's my cuddly buddy, always there.
With gentle snores, he dreams away,
In his own little dachshund way.

Dougie, my faithful and furry friend,
You'll be by my side until the very end.
Through thick and thin, in laughter and tears,
You'll always hold a special place, my dear.

So here's to Dougie, my dachshund so sweet,
With a heart full of love, he can't be beat.
Forever we'll be, through thick and thin,
My best friend Dougie, let the adventures begin!

Sienna Britton (8)

When I Feel Sick

When I feel sick, my mummy is there,
With her special magic, she takes to my care.
She has a smile that brightens my day,
Chasing the clouds and making them sway.

Her hugs are like blankets, warm and tight,
They make me feel safe, just like the night.
She tells me stories and sings me a song,
With her by my side, I can't go wrong.

Her laughter is like medicine, it heals my pain,
Like a rainbow after the rain.
She makes me giggle, she makes me grin,
With her silly jokes and a playful spin.

When I'm feeling down, she brings me cheer,
With games and toys, she makes me veer
Into a world of fun and delight,
Where laughter and joy take flight.

She brings me soup, she brings me tea,
Taking care of me, just like a queen bee.

Her love is like magic, it makes me feel strong,
With her by my side, I can sing along.

She's my superhero, my mummy so dear,
With her, I have nothing to fear.
In her embrace, I find comfort and peace,
Her love for me will never cease.

So, when I'm sick, I know she'll be near,
To wipe away my worries and dry my tear.
With her special magic, she cheers me up,
My mummy's love fills my heart's cup.

Marwah Qasir (10)

A Journey Through The Mind's Laboratory

As you walk inside your mind, waiting anxiously
To see what's in your head, thankfully
All the cells light up your path of fantasy
To blind the hate, the despair, the agony
Powering your hidden alchemy

As you look to the left, a test tube of your thoughts
Your memory, and your movements
Then you stare down into a void full of your
feelings
The anger when you're not heard or your point
can't be proven

Your eyes focus in on a tube, as delicate as the tip
of a tooth
As a steaming liquid takes you back to your
memories and your youth
And forever, it feels, you are left stuck in a vortex
and its complexity

But with the drip of a mixture, the memories are
just pictures
And you're brought back to the forgotten truth

Now, there are figures around you,
Only one-tenth of your size, but together, a giant
they make
As now you know the brain's potential to perform
and supply
Is like a mirror faced with an earthquake
It never breaks, and will only multiply

You stroll into a darkened room, yet everything
seems so lively and bright
Yet then you see a model of the brain, and you
pause to think, and to think you are alright
Would be wrong, as set against your own brain in
a ring
Is like a stand-off between your love and the fright
That floods you and takes over your body
An unfair fight.

Charlie Cook (10)

Pets

My pets are all amazing and fun
And I simply love every single one.
I have some hairy, hairy tarantulas
And one of the many is called Dracula.
I have cute little kittens and cats
And some always-hungry mice and rats.
I have lizards and chameleons, always in disguise
And lots of birds - one of which is an owl, very wise.
I have a few cute rabbits and a few cute bunnies
And some very long snakes with some very
long tummies.
I have some awesome fish in a lot of bowls
and tanks
And some ponies and horses behind doors of
wooden planks.
I have adorable puppies and cute, cute dogs
And lots of non-poisonous frogs.
I have some energetic iguanas, bouncing high
and low
And some calm tortoises that always go slow.
I have cute guinea pigs that often hide because I'm
in sight

And cute, cute hamsters but it's a pity they come out at night.
I have lots of cute gerbils in big-spaced cages
And some big soft chinchillas who live for ages.
I have a lot, lot, lot, lot more, that I haven't mentioned yet
Because I think that you'll find they're inappropriate for a pet.
My pets are all amazing and fun
And I simply love every single one.

Katie Swillman (8)

Somebody Called Anger

Some say he's forged in the dark pits of hell,
And has lingered there,
enchanted by a looming spell,
Looked down at and being called all kinds of weird,
But little do they know he'll soon be feared.

He prays for the day of his sweet revenge,
And the lost power that he has yet to avenge,
Of burning flames and barbaric actions,
That leads to unbearably rude reactions.

Finally, he manages to break the chains,
In which he has been marked with painful stains,
And sets to wreak havoc on innocent souls,
To achieve his menacing, evil goals.

He creeps up the spines of the helpless weak,
And taunts them into saying things
they would never dare to speak,
Just to fuel his burning desire,
Of the world being engulfed in ash and fire.

Then one day a flood of sorrow and regret,
Tore at his heartstrings making him fret,
For the fire in his soul was slowly quenched,
And the evil glare in his eyes was finally drenched.

He knelt on the ground and let out a wail,
Suddenly going very pale,
For when he looked up,
there was nothing in his path,
But death, destruction, war and wrath.

Fahad Hamid (11)

The Incandescent Heart

The volcano rested in utter serenity,
It had no idea about the upcoming calamity,
Silently dozing, calmly slumbering,
Everything was at peace, no rumbling.

A muffled yawn escaped the volcano's mouth,
It had awoken from its rest,
from here everything went south,
Growling, prowling, it was ready for war,
Strategising and scheming
for the upcoming lava pour.

Bash! With no remorse the volcano was ruthless,
It left everything in its wake clueless,
Its ravenous wrath destroyed everything in its way,
Nothing below would live to see another day.

The vegetation below trembled,
They knew what the lava resembled,
Crestfallen that they would die,
They accepted it was time to say goodbye.

The volcano saw the pain he had caused,
And for a split moment, he paused,
He was eaten with guilt,
His whole world would need to be rebuilt.

Slowly but surely the ground regrew,
The trees swayed peacefully too,
The world was still,
The volcano rested, until...

Lucas Bohara (11)

Different Subjects!

As I lay my head into English
Modal verbs, nouns and pronouns
Grammar, spelling and handwriting
Oh wow! So much to learn
Fiction, biography and a diary
I have a diary!

As I dive through the mathematical world
So many symbols and techniques
Geometry, algebra and trigonometry
Addition and subtraction
Wow! This is interesting
Angles, bar graphs and statistics
Are some of the few things that are here

As I walk into science
Or as I call it, magic
Chemistry, biology and physics
This is making me on top of the world
Experiments, test tubes and results
Are all that makes it so interesting!

As my feelings are all lying on the floor
There is nothing more I would like to do
I went on a journey to suspect some of the
subjects
Maths, English and science
Angles, experiments and nouns!

What is all that about?
I feel amazed to sneak a peak
Through some of the subjects!
Oh, now I feel like I am ready to study
Shh, turn down the sound,
I am studying...

Hiya Kashyap (10)

Life In The Chimney

Opening my eyes to see,
An old building which was tall,
I thought Mother and Father were there in
the big hall,
But all there was were masters six feet tall,
Wearing a gown in small.
"I climb for life."

My mother passed away when I was young,
And my father left me with a hungry tum,
Working with an evil master, surrounded by rum,
With nothing left of my parents, I climb for life.

The master always lies of the amount he owes.
There is always a fire which glows.
"As I climb for life."

Days, months, years passed,
My clothes did not last,
Not seen the moon, stars and sun.
In this dark tunnel, I wait to see the world
"As I climb for life."

Loneliness, darkness, smoke and soot
Surrounded me day after night.
With whom I lived for years.
And had become my best friend.
Within my cage.
"As I climb for life."

Will awake one day to see my wishes are granted.
Alone in the tunnel of dust,
Looking at my black skin.
Becoming thicker, heavier.
With an empty stomach and lungs filled with dust,
Higher and higher, I climb into the narrow tunnel.
As I climbed for life.

Dhanusshan Ponnambalam (12)

At The Beach, The Sea Is Mad!

As the intimidating, merciless monster crept up
on the innocent shore,
The sound of a gentle lapping leapt into a
rumbling roar.
Waves crash and splash vigorously through
a mighty storm,
Its white horses delicately gallop together
in a swarm.
At the beach the sea is mad,
Teasing the sand, changing the land.

Shadows dance beneath the depths of the
unforgiving ocean,
The taunting tides tease the sand in a
strange motion.
They shout and bang, carving artwork on the
damp rocks,
Breaching through every wall and stone protecting
the docks.
At the beach the sea is mad,
Crashing on rocks, changing the land.

Glistening diamonds dance majestically over the
blue Atlantic,
It's like the crystal-blue water all of a sudden
starts to panic,
It's full of myth and magic,
It's cruel and sometimes tragic.
Underwater creatures from north to south,
It doesn't have a tongue, but it can swallow
through its mouth.
At the beach the sea is mad,
Teasing the sand, changing the land.

Isla Roberts (11)

Sinister Sloths

Beware of the sleepy sloths, they will trick you
Into thinking they are small and cute,
But while their cuteness seems real, it turns out
it's not true
As actually they are hairy brutes.

Beware of the sleepy sloths, they will scratch you
With long sharp nails,
Their lethal scratching never fails
To pierce three insects with one paw.

While they are phenomenally slow,
Evolution unfortunately decided long ago
That the sloths are coming for us.

As the human race could never prepare,
For these sloths that caught us unaware.
Their laziness is seeping through our minds,
Past our curtains and through our blinds.

While we stare at the TV screen,
Suddenly we are lost in our lazy daydreams.

The human race could never have detected,
This attack from the sloths, (very unexpected).

So beware these 'sleepy' sloths,
As they will lazify you when you turn your back.
I warn you now to protect yourself,
From the launch of the brutal lazy brain attack.

Harriet Brett (10)

The Corridor

In the darkness, I wander alone
Down a corridor, I've never known
The air is thick
The silence is loud
As I tread upon the chilly ground.

The walls around me seem too close
With every step, my fear grows
That something's watching,
Never leaving.

The flickering lights, the creaking floor
Make me wish I'd never stepped through that door.
The shadows danced, the whispers called
As I slowly made my way down the hall.

I try to move faster, but my feet won't obey
As I stumble and trip, and lose my way
The fear grips me tighter, the panic takes hold
As I struggle to escape this terror so cold.

Finally, I see the end in sight
But as I reach the door, it shuts tight

I'm trapped in this corridor of fear
With no escape, no one to hear.

I scream and shout, but no one replies
As I face my fate with terror-filled eyes
In this corridor, I'm all alone
And here, I fear, I'll never find my way
Home.

Kailyn-Faith Liley (13)

My Craziest Day At School

I woke up late and missed the bus,
I had to run and catch a fuss.
I forgot my homework and my lunch,
I felt like I was out of touch.
I reached the school and saw a crowd,
They were all screaming very loud.
I pushed my way and saw the scene,
Giant spaceship on the green.
It opened up and out came some
Strange creatures that looked like gum.
They said they came from far away,
And wanted to learn and play.
They asked me if I could be their guide,
And show them how to have fun inside.
I agreed and took them to my class,
And hoped they wouldn't make a mess.
They were curious and eager to know
About everything from maths to snow.
They made friends with everyone they met
And even taught us their alphabet.
They said they had to go back soon

But they would come again next June.
They gave me a hug and a gift
And thanked me for the lift.
They boarded their ship and waved goodbye
And flew away into the sky.
I was left with a smile and a surprise
And a crazy story for my eyes!

Aradhya Aggarwal (9)

Flesh, Blood, And Bones

Flesh, blood, and bones,
We see you every day.
And when we meet in Davy Jones,
You won't have gone away.

For every pirate fights 'til death,
Until the end of our service,
Until we take one last breath,
Until we sink below the ocean's surface.

We may search golden shores,
For a priceless treasure chest.
We may be greedy for gold galore,
And 'til we get them, we'll not rest.

You cannot judge us in any way,
There are too many of our kind.
Some are greedy, night and day,
Keeping whatever they find.

But there are cruel and fair ones of us,
Who never kill one unarmed,
Or don't torture those who make a fuss,

Of our ghastly appearances, although
they're unharmed.

You can either choose,
To be one of us, but be warned,
If you're captured, they'll never set you loose.
Or to be a normal person, to us, forlorn.

Belinda Kong (10)

The Song Of The Birch

In your branches, flocks of birds perch
Your silver coat shines bright in the moonlight.

Your branches long to kiss the sky
You're rooted to the ground and yet you
seem to fly
Your spirit soars above cities and towns

Above man-made temples and natural grounds
Looking for the perfect sound to make your
branches billow

The song of a sweeping, elegant willow.
You long for this sound to heal your soul

You were heartbroken in the past
From savage metal beasts
Stealing your song.
And nothing else can make it come back
Apart from the beautiful willow
To make your branches billow.

Then all the squirrels will know
About the billowing birch
Which grows and sways in the wind.
It's a beautiful song that sounds so sweet
Flutters through the air like a newborn
bird's tweet.

Its song is back
Its heart is healed
And it gives his thanks
To all the world
Who helped him
Find the wonderful willow
That made his branches billow.

Maya Pal (8)

The Winter Star

A series of notes, wailing and yowling
The sky is bright with the Winter Star prowling.
It sits on the night, conductor of light,
Instructing the stars to sing with might.
Brightest of all, never to fall,
The Winter Star watches over the sky.
It conducts the notes, low and high.
And what a beautiful sound, oh my, oh my!
It's guiding a choir, an orchestra - no!
It's creating a fantastical, musical show!
With drama and love all sung in your voice,
The stars are above making a choice, of
Comedy, tragedy. Laughter and tears,
All are expressed if you have ears.
Listen up close, and on silent nights,
When the dark is lit up with starry lights,
You might hear a sky song, a beautiful sound.
Yes, listen up close, for they don't sing loud.
Made up of melodic, harmonious talent,
Both meek and mad, most certainly gallant.

So take a curtsey, take a bow,
How the Winter Star does it, I just don't know how.

Serena Williams (11)

The Library

Today, at the library,
From her big shelves,
The books were calling me...
To read them.

And every book
Had a different and
Interesting content and
My eyes were drawn
To a thick book
With a leather cover and
A distinct mark.

It's like he's calling me,
By name, desperately!
"Open me!" and I open it.

I woke up in a completely different world
Full of magic,
With mythical and brightly coloured characters.
Everything was fascinating, unique and
Made me forget who I am.

The characters were waiting for me,
Holding my hand and
They showed me unprecedented places
That left me speechless.

That's how I wake up to reality and
I saw that I'd read many chapters and
I can say that:
The library is a unique world,
Charmed, full of mysteries and life.

Ayinoor Murray (11)

My Don't Do Poem

Don't
Don't do,
Don't, do
Don't do that.

Don't be annoying,
Don't disrupt the cat.
Don't make a mess,
Don't do this and don't do that.
Who do they think I am?
Some kind of fool?

One day they'll say
Don't put a shrew in my stew
Don't put a mouse in my house
Don't move my groove
Don't pick up a vole on its stroll.

Don't stop the teddy trying to turn on the telly
And don't ride a BMX through a DVD.
Don't make a rat run from a cat
Don't hit the fat rat for the cat

Don't make a sound in the round crown
And don't throw at mice
Don't throw rice at mice.

Don't what?
Don't throw rice at mice
Don't what?
Don't throw rice at mice
Who do they think I am?
Some kind of fool?

Abel Naidoo (8)

Victoria Veil

A tale of a girl who rang a bell for eternity

Victoria was not an ordinary girl,
She had long, cascading hair which ended in curls,
Her shrivelled face showed no disgrace,
The golden bell dingled in its space,
Her chin held high, and nose tickled pink,
You were sure not to even take a blink,
And now I give to you her ghastly fate,
About which I sorrowfully relate.

It started with a treasured bell,
That she clinked and gave a yell,
Her butler came whizzing around,
To her service, he is found,
Plates piled high, and a weary face,
Her orders were answered with such grace,
However, this was not the case,
Her orders were snubbed without a trace.

Her bad-tempered manner was one to beware,
But her snobby parents were not so aware,
Day by day, week by week,

Her outrage made her cry out and shriek,
Her worn-out bell and aching hand,
She grew old and frail and still lived grand,
The butlers long gone, on holiday perhaps,
She rang the bell until her hand collapsed.

Mimi Sun (11)

Explorers

Explorers are kind,
They are quick, they are clever
They have ships, they have maps,
They never say never.

They're heroes and fighters,
They find exciting new places
But they're famous and noisy,
And cover up the faces

Of people who were first.
Who don't speak English, or look white
But are people like us,
And have all of their right

To be declared heroes.
Because history is made up of them
And it only shows the winners.
Because to be explorers you don't need to win.

Exploring is finding,
And discovering, and trying new things.

A pretty old building,
A bird with colourful wings.

Your map can be old thanks to a tea bag
And your ship can be made of an old
cardboard box.

Because explorers are kind,
They are quick, they are clever
And to be an explorer
You just need to be curious forever.

Caterina Williams (12)

Three Days In The Life Of The Chough

Day one
The morning sunrise glowing across the sea
Making me awe-struck by its beauty
As I hunt for food for my littlies
The flowers blossom turning into beautiful lilies
Oh, isn't the sun nice today?
People out in their gardens, happily weeding away
Oh, this is a day in the life of the chough

Day two
Busy bees pollinating flowers
Ants carrying leaves
Little birds learning to fly
And managing to achieve
Oh, isn't the sun nice today?
People out in their gardens, happily weeding away
Oh, this is a day in the life of the chough

Day three
Seagulls soaring through the sky

Taking a girl's ice cream and making her cry
The tide coming in and soaking tourists' feet
Loving the nice gentle heat
Oh, isn't the sun nice today?
People out in their gardens, weeding away
Oh, this is a day in the life of a chough.

Sennen Davis (10)

Unleashing Our Power Rap

I am special and can change the world
Want to help nature even if it sounds absurd.
Look what I can do
If I try and push through
'Cause I am special and can change the world.

You are special and can change the world
You can do anything even if it's in a dream world
You should see what you can do
If you try and push through
'Cause you are special and can change the world.

We are special and can change the world
We should do anything to make our
dreams emerge
We should see what we can do
If we try and push through
'Cause we are special and can change the world.

Everyone is special and can change the world
We should surely use our intelligence and
everything we've learned
We all know what we can do

If we try and push through
'Cause everyone is special and can change
the world!

Janna Oyedeji (10)

A Typical Girl's Life

Act prim and proper
Show no emotion
Be someone's perfect daughter
Never make a commotion
Then get wed at the altar
But just as a selection
They'll later throw you like a toy
Leaving you ready to destroy

That's how it always was
Nobody used to fight or be a nurse
We all were stuck there, at our worst
Nobody stood up for us
Because we were deemed as worthless
Just a piece of rubbish to throw around
Like a dictator, hungry for the crown

But a revelation happened
From out of the ground
The women made a loud sound
And the power began to shake
Causing a war outbreak

Yet during this war, the world began to change
The others all thought it was strange
But we stood up tall
Making them all feel small
They all couldn't believe what they saw
We weren't living a typical girl's life anymore.

Mahpary Ghorbany

The Wonderful World Of Books

It helps you to enter a spectacular world,
A world full of fantasy and horror,
It takes you to another planet, another dimension,
A place that is completely unworldly.
It allows you to escape the horrors of reality
And enter a heavenly world,
A world full of mystery and myths.

You'll get addicted,
You'll be curled up in an armchair,
With a book in your hands,
You'll love it, you truly will.

My obsession started when I was very young,
I discovered this incredible pack of parchment,
It was smothered in words,
That opened the door to an unrealistic world.

I was amazed
And day after day,
I visited the world,

More and more each time.

Pretty soon, I was a regular visitor,
And books took me as a regular customer
And to this day,
Not a day goes by,
That I don't pay a visit to the wonderful
world of books.

Tanudi Vitharana (11)

Divided

The sound of bombs, the cries of pain,
The horror of battle lay plain.
Brothers and sisters, once united,
Now on opposite sides divided.

In fields of blood and endless strife,
Humanity's darkest side comes to life.
Soldiers fight for their beliefs,
Families left to bear the grief.

The broken cities, the shattered dreams,
The cost of war beyond what it seems.
Fathers, mothers, children lost,
A terrible price paid at a terrible cost.

Yet in the aftermath a glimmer of hope,
A chance for peace and love to elope.
For every heart that's still intact,
A chance to rebuild and to act.

So let's put down our guns and start to heal,
Let love and compassion be our shield.

For, in the end, war's destructive sway,
Only leaves behind the echoes of death and
dismay.

Sophia Venters (10)

Your Story

These are mere words;
You make them come alive.
You breathe life and spirit into them.
You live in the stories, we solely write them.
Each word,
Each paragraph,
Each page,
Crafted to make your heart race,
To make you sob,
To make you sigh with relief,
To make you think and create.
I am not a writer.
I transport you to magical lands,
To wherever your imagination takes you.
I am not a writer.
I am your companion on the journey of a lifetime,
Through jungles and lakes and mountains.
I am not a writer.
I am a fighter; my weapon is this pen,
Which can impose such rage, such harrowing
misery.

Or at times can light up your day, provide such comfort and joy.

So, allow yourself to lose yourself in a story,
To get trapped between the pages of a book,
Just remember,
We are not your writers.
You write your own story.

Selin Erdogan (12)

Concrete Jungle

I ran, I ran until the grass was no more
I ran, I ran till I came across a door
On one side flowers tangled like hair
What could be on the other side, could it
be just as fair?
I opened the door and stepped inside
Hearing my footsteps echoing behind
Oh, jungle of concrete what are you?
Where is the past and what is your present?
Taller than trees you are, but are you content?
Covered by the grey, barely can be seen
Who are you and what do you mean?
But then look the sun rises
And then the jungle is full of surprises
Suddenly you see life not like any other
Getting up perfectly with no bother
Nobody has seen me, Jungle
The species just goes on in their perfect huddle
But then one stops and looks at me

I scream and run, back to my Birch Trees
Then I realised there is hope in the
Concrete Jungle.

Ziona Kyere-Diabour (12)

The Great Family Poem

Families big or small
You've got to love them all
DNA or friends
Together through the bends
Caring each day
Showing the way

Carers make an impact
I know that for a fact
Mum and Dad, a prime example
Definitely a good sample
Adopter, foster and more
Making a difference we can't ignore

Grannies make good nannies
Even with bad knees
Aunties, often smarties
Helping with the parties
Whether far or near
They're always there to cheer

Not rosy all the time
May sometimes be sour as lime
Brothers play with joy
But argue over a toy

But though things fall apart
Or even break the heart
Whatever the weather
We always stick together.

Walter Ebam (8)

The Academy Of Poetry And Rhyme

As the Academy of Poetry opens its doors,
The staff and teachers set out on their chores.
Papers and pencils they hand out,
As the children start writing without a doubt.

The spiky-haired wizard writes about spells galore,
The elegant princess writes about a prince at
her door.
A brave knight writes about dragons and battles,
The sweet little boy writes about his toy that
rattles.

Why not take a hand at writing and join the
Academy of Poetry and Rhyme?
At least come and visit, it'll not be a waste of time!
Write anything, whether it's about a princess
or a knight,
Or even spooky monsters that give you quite
a fright!

Then, at dawn, when the Academy closes its doors,
The student happily goes, thinking, *I can't wait to write some more.*

Dea B (11)

Who Cried Wolf

Who cried wolf on a winter's night,
A hollow scream and a ghostly shout,
A call for help,
A life snuffed out,
Tragedy is all about.

I came a-running,
My gun a-cocked,
Into the night I ran,
To find a body,
To kill a wolf,
To find the truth tonight.

In the woods,
I found the wolf,
The tables turned tonight.

The wolf was hurt,
The unknown victim had run unharmed,
It's eyes a glowing amber,
They took me in a trance,

She showed me her child,
Her baby wolf-cub.

The beauty of nature,
True to me now,
I now know,
That at any day,
I will give my life for hers,
The wolf I found that night,
That is the reason I am alive.

Anoushka Singh-Dhami (11)

Recipe For The Old And Wise

Take:
The alabaster white of snow,
The bushiness of a mountain sheep's fur,
And the length of a boa constrictor,
For his hair and moustache,

Take:
The texture of corrugated iron,
The roughness of a tree's bark,
And the creases of a paper aeroplane,
For his skin,

Take:
The hiding of the Lost City,
The chocolate brown of a bog,
And the dryness of Death Valley,
For his lips.

Take:
The emerald green of grass,
The thoughtfulness of time itself,

And the weariness of a sloth,
For his eyes.

Take:
The wisdom of Dumbledore,
The faith of a patient teacher,
And the compassion of a good Samaritan,
For the advice I need for life.

Harry Marshall

The Lion

Lion! Lion! Sparkling high, in the heart of the sky,
What an appealing sight comes to thee's eye,
What has the lord of animals come to see
In our faithful human society?

Behind the brightness of thy mane
Is the cleverness of the brain?
Will a single petulant scheme
Make thine's mind scream?

Your heart is made of gold
And it is a story untold,
How did the first of your ancestors
Roam the earth free?

Will an anchor be able to defeat thee?
Or a thousand bullets, that hurt thine eyes to see?
The sapphires that shine in thine's teeth,
Enough to trick a thief!

Lion! Lion! Sparkling high, in the diamond of the sky,
What an appealing sight comes to thee's eye,

What has the lord of animals come to see?
In our faithful human society?

Ania Dave (9)

Autumn Slumber

Leaping through time,
Into an everlasting cycle,
As life fades away,
Autumn time is here.

The season of colour begins,
When temperatures decrease,
The time when green turns to the colours
scarlet, amber and medallion yellow,
To create an exquisite landscape.

Hibernation is due,
And in addition, metamorphoses,
Many animals hear an exhausting call,
As they yawn, yawn, yawn.

Little by little,
The lively nature I know,
Dissolves into thin air,
For nothing stays the same.
As I watch the colours and liveliness
change in autumn with awe,

I realise its annual routine,
Life fades away,
Only to bring more life.

Dhara Wickramasekara (11)

Summer Shock

Perched atop a floating flamingo,
The blazing sun scorches my sweaty chest.
Glancing back to the busy beach,
Gazing upon picturesque palm trees.
Swaying like dancers to the music of the ocean,
Their whiskered coconuts beat out the rhythm.
Perspiring profusely in the stifling heat,
Sunburn blisters my body, my head hurting.
Blinding me by the moment,
The shimmering sun sizzles my eyes.
A jingle jangle catches my ear,
I turn my head.
Ice-cold ice cream catches my eye.
The scent of velvety chocolate lures me in.
Promptly paddling shore-wards, focused on my
sweet treat,
I notice not the shadowy shape beneath my vessel.
Near to shore, swimmers scream and
screamers run.
Not knowing why, I turn and spy
The fin...

Peyton Ormond (9)

Trench Deadlock

T rench warfare was supposed to be a temporary measure,

R eally, this was unexpected,

E verything tastes terrible,

N ow the water has petrol in it,

C learly, the bacon is cold and greasy too,

H ow much longer can we last on the frontlines?

W e're all risking our lives here,

A nd we know that a sniper's bullet could just end our lives,

R etaliate,

F or soon we may break out of this trench deadlock,

A nd my back hurts, but I can't afford to take a rest,

R epelling the enemies, we finally are out of these trenches,

E uphoria, for we have won the war, we can finally take a breather, but for how long will this peace last?

Abid Md Khalid Ibne (11)

Try Your Best

Try your best, don't give up,
Even when you find it tough,
Just remember you're enough
And when you think I'm done,
Please don't give up, because you're fine.
What if I say, "Just try, try, try
And you will live a great life."
Just try, it's as easy as that,
If you can try, you will be successful in life.
I mean, look at your mum or dad,
They have a great life,
Can you guess why?
Because they tried!
As easy as that,
If you try, you will love your life
And you want that, don't you?
So guess what, you have to try!
Try your best and don't give up,
Just remember you're enough
Just try.
The note to you is just try

And you'll be fine in life.
Just try.

Mollie Conneely (9)

No One Ever Compares To Him

He was a light to the world.
He had a heart of gold.
He was kind to both young and old.
No one ever compares to him.

He'd give you a warm embrace,
Welcoming you with a smile on his face.
You'd be amazed by all his grace.
No one ever compares to him.

He was noble, just and fair.
He was generous and loved to share.
He treated everyone with love and care.
No one ever compares to him.

He would let grudges go,
Forgiving even his greatest foes,
Making your love for him grow.
No one ever compares to him.

He was a man so humble,
And he is the best example.
Prophet Muhammad (PBUH)* is my role model.
No one ever compares to him.

*Peace be upon him

Nusayba Ahmed (11)

What If...?

What was the question that made it all happen?
What two words make your life what it is?
What are the words that begin all new things?
What if makes the world go round?

What if we made a story of wizards?
What if we made a little room that moves?
What if we could make people fly?
What if we put a man on the moon?
What if we made a machine that makes fire?
What if we made schools where children
can learn?

These are the questions that seem basic
But are revolutionary.
What if is the foundation of life,
So forget the facts and ask yourself, what if?

What if I made a difference by simply asking,
what if?

Ishani Halford (11)

The Magic Gecko

T he magic gecko is very majestic.

H e can make you a billionaire.

E very day, he's making people happy.

"M y new pet," said the girl,

"A nd it's magic!" she also said.

"G oing to save the world," she said happily.

I t can fly, shoot lasers and it is very cute.

C ute, yes it is, but it is very vicious sometimes.

G eckos are very scaly and small.

E veryone should love them.

C an the gecko go invisible? Of course!

K eep it safe so that you can stay safe!

O kay, that's all about the magic gecko for now.

Jessica Neale (10)

King Henry VIII

So many wives,
But who does he want?
So much hesitation,
Who will he choose?

Catherine of Aragon,
Anne Boleyn,
Jane Seymour,
Anne of Cleves,
Catherine Howard or
Catherine Parr?

Catherine of Aragon,
She didn't have a boy,
Divorced!

Anne Boleyn,
Had a girl,
Beheaded!

Jane Seymour,
Finally had a boy,
But died in childbirth.

Catherine Howard,
Couldn't bear Henry and his children,
Divorced!

Anne Of Cleves,
Had a girl,
Beheaded!

Catherine Parr,
No children,
Survived!

Molly Hind (10)

Inside My Wonderful Dream

Inside my wonderful dream...
A unicorn appears as soon as I shut my eyes,
As sparkly as the billions of stars in the night sky,
Galloping and glittering,
A wonder to my mind.

Inside my wonderful dream...
Dragons fly high, near the cloudy night moon,
Like something you could only dream of,
Roaring and gliding,
Wonderful moments that only appear in an
imagination full of adventures.

Inside my wonderful dream...
Giants' gloopy snot appears as a green waterfall,
As slimy as a slug or snail,
Dripping and drooping,
Not something you'd like to come across.

Inside my wonderful dream...
It's something you'd enjoy,

Just close your eyes and imagine,
No more worries at all.

Lilly Whiston (10)

I Met A Cockatoo

I went to the zoo,
And saw a cockatoo.
The cockatoo said to me,
"Can you climb that tree?
Because up there is crumble
That will make your tummy rumble."
I did what the cockatoo asked me to do,
But halfway up I needed a poo.
I jumped down
And saw a clown,
But I couldn't stop to say hello
Because I really had to go.
So I went to the loo,
And did what I needed to do.
Then I started to climb the tree again,
I said, "Hello cockatoo, it's me again."
So I climbed and got the crumble
Then the cockatoo started to mumble,
And, of course, I ate the crumble.
It really made my tummy rumble

So I gobbled up some more -
It was really good for sure!

Lewis Ramsay (8)

Be Grateful

Adventures are fun and exciting,
But don't think just about you,
Think about others too!

On the journey of your life,
Be as soft as a dove,
With the people you love.
Face your fears,
Face the thing that haunts you for years.

Make new friends on the way.
But don't forget
To make the old ones stay.
True friends are the ones to keep,
Not fakes that leap away.

Treasure everything you have:
Your house, your family,
Your legs you walk with,
Your hands you touch with,
Your eyes you see with,
Both ears to hear with,

And your heart to feel with.
The clothes you wear,
The food on the table.
These things may sound simple,
But they make us healthy and happy!

Alexandra Rusu (10)

Poor Little Animals

Poor little animals,
Thinking what to do?
Poor little animals,
Their homes being polluted by you.

Poor little animals.
Lost and sad,
Poor little animals.
Starting to get mad.

Poor little animals,
Fleeing from their homes,
Poor little animals,
Bumping into garden gnomes.

Poor little animals,
Are begging in vain,
Poor little animals,
Feeling like Ukraine.

Poor little animals,
Life is unfair.

Poor little animals,
Even for the bears.

Poor little animals,
Think about them,
Poor little animals,
Time to save them!

Nihira Paravastu (10)

My Best Friend

My best friend has no hair
But I still know they are there

My best friend is nameless
But could be famous!

My best friend is all I need
They're way better than a weed

My best friend doesn't speak
But they know so many words they could go
on for a week

My best friend has no face
But they take me all over the place

My best friend makes no sound
But if I'm lost I know I'll be found

My best friend may go crazy and lose their mind
But they are always very kind

People may give me funny looks
When they find out my best friends are books.

Ditty Jones (9)

Volcano

Volcanoes are mountains slumbering like babies.

They are as tall as skyscrapers and as peaceful
As a calm sea.

The mountain's belly rumbles loudly, and lava and
Ash erupts from its mouth.

The lava is as red as Mars and as hot as the
Centre of the Earth.

The ash is as dark as outer space and falls
From the sky.

The lava eats everything in its path until there is
Nothing left.

The lava hardens into rock and awaits the next
Explosion.

The volcano is now an old man and goes back
To being a peaceful, slumbering giant.

Sophia Junglas (8)

A Soldier's Goodbye

Atop the watch tower, the wet wind blows,
The brutal Picts are our foes.
We fight, we fight, we fight with might,
Day after day, night after night.

The wind bites our faces, the rain licks them clean,
The squelching mud, in place of the green.
Bodies pile up in an amorphous mass,
Our adversaries and our own, all dead, alas.

The clouds are bruising, the lightning strikes,
Our rivals charge with swords and spikes.
Screams and shouts deafen my ears,
I roar, I lunge, I dodge the spears.

Abruptly, a searing pain in my back,
I stumble, I fall, I see pitch-black.
I think of my home and imagine the sky,
I pray to the Lord, I say goodbye.

Alejandro Kidel (10)

When The Fishes Flew

On this one day, the sea fishes flew,
The shady night sky was dark blue.

My calm, kind mind was feeling free,
As fishes start to glow, it's cool to see.

Fishes felt the Earth's gentle breeze,
Only then they wouldn't start to freeze.

The night stars lit our gloomy world,
Fishes air-swam with minds uncurled.

They poofed their heads up in clouds,
As a star comes, soon there are crowds.

With silky, beautiful bettas filling the sky,
If any other fish come, I don't see why!

Witnessing this is like a magnificent dream,
After viewing, I'll use it as my bedroom theme.

Farah Karim (10)

The Demon

I am the sinister demon
The one who will dictate your state.
Roll the dice of life and death
But be prepared to meet your fate.

I am the merciless menace
Descend to me I must pray.
I will send chills down your neck,
But I might let you have your day.

You won't ever win
The ominous clouds will mist your mind.
You won't even know what is happening
But do not expect me to be kind.

This is your one final caution.
Fail to heed my simple warning
And I'll freeze your limbs to ice,
You'll be as good as dead by morning!

Lily Cobb (10)

Callous Comet

When the correct time strikes
The diabolical comet will fall,
With no indications whatsoever
Besides its shrieking call

It appears at supersonic speed,
A sight you'll never forget,
It's surrounded by rock, dust and embers,
And has little to no regret

No one will ever know where it came from,
But some think it was born from a star,
But little did they know that the comet was
plotting from afar...

It overflows with envy,
It obliterates with a gasp,
It desolates anything trapped
In... it's... powerful... grasp.

Lennon Round (9)

At School

At school, we have collective worship in the hall.
At school, at break time, we play football.

At school, we have play.
Some lessons, we sculpt clay.

At school, you make good friends.
You also use equipment like glue and a pen.

At school, we do learning.
That is how you get good earnings.

At school, we go on trips.
For our play, we learn scripts.

At school, we have nice lunch.
Tastes so good, *munch, munch, munch*.

At school, we do maths.
Always stay on the right path.

Zayden Cavanagh (9)

What's On The Menu?

It's Tuesday!
So, I picked up the phone
And they ask, "What would you like?"
We collect our red or blue boxes.
We see the glorious sight.
We smell the mouth-watering freshness.

Time for the first bite,
Mmmmmmmm!
Sweet, soft dough,
Covered in a silky layer of red sauce.
A smooth, golden string stretches from my mouth.
Flaming-red circles of magnificence,
Tingles every one of my tastebuds.
Finally, the crust
To finish it off
But it's never enough.
I need more, more and more!

Riley Jones (9)

Karate Day

First, I woke up in the morning,
To not get any warning.
Next, I got dressed
And my clothes were pressed.
Then, I sat in my car,
To go to karate, that was very far!
So, I went to my match,
And sat on the number 11 batch.
I had butterflies in my tummy,
But at least there were my grandparents
and mummy.
They cheered me up by clapping,
And my butterflies stopped flapping.
I won and came in number one,
And it was really really fun!
I absolutely loved my trophy,
And my mum absolutely loved her coffee.
I went home and had a bowl of ice cream,
And my trophy was my life's dream.

Shaurya Holkar

In My Garden

In my garden, observe the trees,
In my garden, I observe the bees,
Stems, leaves and roots
Flowers, branches and fruits
What a diverse place to be,
So come here and see.

I start at one.
But I soon, have it all outdone.

In my house, I feed some ants,
And they seem to want to stay
So let it be that way
That's all I would say.

On sugar, they feast
If it was meat,
They would truly be a beast.

In my room, I like to write
That's what I was doing before
My love of writing poems grows more and more,
Lots, of ideas I have in store.

Susnato Mallick (9)

My School Years

In 2021 I was in Year 1,
I had a lot of fun and I learnt a sum.

In 2022 I was in Year 2,
I had no clue what to do.

In 2023 I am in Year 3,
I'm learning more about me,
And growing like a tree.

In 2024 I'll be in Year 4,
And I am sure...
I will know a lot more!

In 2025 I'll be in Year 5,
I'll dive straight in and be sure to thrive!

In 2026 I will be in Year 6,
I'll learn new tricks and go on many trips.
I'll pass on good tips to the rest of the school
And get ready to rule my secondary school.

Aarav Sharma (8)

Are We There Yet?

Tick-tock!
I watch down the seconds on the clock,
Until we are ready to dock.
Are we there yet?
Slish-slosh!
I watched the tide form,
As I head into my dorm.
Are we there yet?
Swish-swash!
The Brits are posh,
None of them speak tosh.
Are we there yet?
Clack! Thump!
We are at the port of the South East coast,
And no need to boast
But we are finally here!
O' Windrush rush,
All aboard, need to be hush
Because its legacy cannot be crushed!

Maliha Mohiuddin (11)

Winter Obsession

There's a chill lingering in the air
People want to venture to their lair
We want something hot
Maybe it's cooking in the pot

The leaves aren't there
The trees are bare
But the nights are growing longer
We have less time to ponder

We snuggle up in our beds
Yet, our noses and toes still feel dead
We turn on our heaters
They should look a little neater

We ignore the mould
We just don't want to be cold
We get a hot drink
Careful not to spill it in the sink

Yet when summer comes
We want to feel numb

We ask, where are you winter
Oh, where are you winter?

Yasmin Abdullah (11)

Writer's Block

I hate writer's block
It doesn't rock
It fills my brain
What a pain
What am I to do?

Why did it come?
It makes me glum
My brain sticks
It just won't click
What am I to do?

I just can't rhyme
Or write on the lines
No new ideas
It's like I've had 10 beers
What am I to do?

I need your help
Or my brain will melt
The deadline is soon
My brain's on the moon

What am I to do?
Here is my poem for you
It's just going to have to do
What a struggle
I'm in a muddle
Love from a writer with writer's block!

Isla McGrath (10)

The Power Of The Poem

Today I went to the loo in the zoo...
And then I went, "Atchoo!" in my shoe
And then I mixed mustard with my custard...

I thought, *I won't give my dog a log*
I won't give the Norse any sauce
I won't give a nurse a curse

I will not let my face turn red in a race at the place
I will give the cook a book
I will watch the light at night

But...

I won't
Give the cat the bat
Or give the hawk any chalk
And I will not put blue glue in my white shoe.

Larissa Armstrong (10)

Who Is There?

Who is there when you're feeling small,
With their kind reminders to stand proud and tall?

Who is there when times get tough?
Their winning grin is just enough!

Who is there when you're feeling down?
They turn your frown the right way around.

Who is there to lend a hand,
When things are tricky to understand?

Who do you seek when you need some advice?
They're glad to help and always nice.

Who is there when things go wrong?
To show you how to be wise and strong.

Friends are!

Ayla Hodson (8)

My Weekend

I wake up and I realise
I have no school today!
I go and grab my football kit
And run downstairs to play.

I go home, have a snack
And go to play some cricket,
I cross my fingers in the car
And hope I get a wicket!

Later in the afternoon
I get my homework finished.
By the time I've got it done,
I'm absolutely famished!

I go upstairs, whip off my clothes
Then hop into the shower.
I put on my comfy pyjamas
And read in bed for hours.

After dinner, I play Nintendo
With my brother in the den.

I go to bed utterly exhausted
Ready to do it all over again!

Finlay Hutchings (9)

Swimming

Water pounds within my ears,
My stomach twists with all my fears.

The race begins with the sound of a gun,
It will not end until I have won.

Doing anything but my best cannot happen,
Especially if I want to be the swim team captain.

A new best time is what I need,
So the other swimmers I will heed.

The pulsing water and the roar of fans
Gets driven out by the voice of a man.

It's familiar and comfortable, telling me to go,
Pushing me onward, not letting me slow.

Amy Atkins (13)

Georgey Dragon

Georgey Dragon chose to potter,
Since the trend was getting hotter,
Dressed in an apron and some gloves,
With the clay, he soon fell in love.

On his birthday Georgey awoke,
Not expecting the wicked joke,
Advancing to the studio,
What he saw turned him cold as snow.

His arch-nemesis, Jefferson,
Moulding mud, beaming like the sun,
Without thought, Georgey leapt at the rogue,
Clothes of clay, no longer in vogue.

Blood, sweat and tears fell to the ground,
Tustling like bulls, so they were found,
By a teacher, who angrily
Kicked them out, a true tragedy.

Maddox Steinberg-Aziz (9)

A Refreshing Treat

Ice cream,
What a delicious treat!
It has a huge gleam,
We love to eat,
It has so much power,
To keep you energised for the whole day,
Make sure you're a lover,
It doesn't taste as boring as grey,
I love it!
It's my #1 best,
It makes my mind lit,
It helps me rest,
Suck! Suck!
Bite! Bite!
Such luck!
It tastes so bright!
We hate vegetables!
Yeah, we do!
My mom says it's edible,
They expect us to chew it,
We love chocolates!

Yeah, we do!
I always have one in my pocket,
My dentist says, "I want one too."

Aaditri Manjunath (9)

Under My Bed

Beneath the tidy surface
Lies a messy land
A pile of musty socks beside
A bucket of old sand.

A pile of old duvets
Creating lumps and bumps
A box near the back wall
Containing several old forgotten Flumps.

Some bottles of used fly spray
Atop a broken toy toad
A can of Coke and Mentos
Which refused to just explode.

Now you know what's down there
You won't come and take a peek
Of what I've hidden under my bed
It's all just so... unique.

Emily Hartness (10)

What Am I?

Fight, fight, fight!
A fierce war flares
On black and white squares.
Armies clash
In a ferocious bash!
Here come the troops
Preparing to form in groups.
Calvary leap and creep
And prepare to reap
On unsuspecting squares.
One is a long-range piece, but nevertheless
It is only worth three troops compared to the rest.
The fort on the other hand is mighty and tall
Prepared for any battle big or small.
The queen commands the army
When all is lost, she remains hardy.
Hip, hip, hooray, the battle is won!
Long live the king for he is the one.

Benjamin Hiseman (9)

Animals

Penguin chicks are incredibly fluffy,
Adult penguins can be very puffy,
Polar bears have a good sense of smell,
In the wild, they do so well.

I'm a monkey, I live at the zoo,
Come up close and I'll entertain you,
I feed my rabbit bananas, carrots and lettuce too,
Sometimes she likes to play peek-a-boo.

Lions are large mighty cats,
That live in the wild and are very fast,
Cheetahs are my favourite big cat,
They're always running so they don't get fat.

Oliver Morgan

Memories

Everyone's memories are their own,
To know how far they've grown,
There are lots of memories you find
And some are even one-of-a-kind.

Some can be sad and upsetting,
Some that you just feel like forgetting,
Some can be happy and delightful,
Some can be scary and frightful.

Memories can be in the past,
Memories can go so fast,
Memories can go so slow,
Memories can always grow.

They just sit there in your head,
Just sitting there till they're read,
One thing you ought to know,
Never let those memories go.

Esme Stone (10)

Penguin Poem

Penguins are funny birds because they cannot fly.
But when it comes to babies
they keep them warm and dry.
They waddle around Antarctica,
smart in black and white
But if they see a killer whale,
they will lose the fight.

They shoot like rockets through the water
whoosh! they are so fast.
A feast of fish must keep them full,
their dinner has to last.
I'd love to be a penguin, they're having such a ball.
The only way they would have more fun is right
here at The Hall.

Theo Neuberger (9)

The Worm That Wore A Hat

The worm that wore a hat
Was eating loads of food
And wriggling around
With an awful attitude

He didn't have a spine
And he didn't have the time
To talk to minibeasts
Too busy gobbling feasts!

He was disgusting and he was slimy
Stinky and stretchy - blimey!

He liked to dance about
He liked to sing and shout
But then he started choking
And he wasn't even joking!

The other worms were kind
And rushed to help him breathe
They helped him feel much better
A good friend is all you need!

D'Angelo Mallam Tait (7)

Phoenix

Red, ochre and yellow,
Wings of molten gold,
King of fabulous fire,
Winner of beauty and bold,
A sign of peace,
That will never cease,
And live forevermore,
Reborn from the ashes,
Making huge splashes,
Is the majestic phoenix,
Burning itself to fix,
Its bare feathers,
In very cold weather,
So it can keep warm,
And then join its swarm,
Lying in the lake,
Wide awake,
As beautiful as a flower,
Fire shimmering everywhere,
When they prepare
To take off

Into the sky,
Waving a wing
To say goodbye.

Chunmay Avyaya Narravula (10)

Kallos

Perfect pink flowers in vine-covered bushes.
A sunset so gorgeous its memories will last forever in my mind.
White and blue buildings stacked upon a lovely land dowsed in reflections of the sun.
The ocean, clear as glass shimmers and shines.
The sky slowly fades from bright and bold orange into deeper than dark purple.
The noise of the waves lapping and flapping as boats run through them is music to my ears.
A calming, serine-like feeling.
It's kallos.

Taylor Hotchkiss (11)

My Toy

When I was a little boy,
My parents bought me a toy,
It was very fun to play with,
And I got it from Smyths,
I really loved it,
Until it got bit,
By a huge, dangerous dog,
The dog bit it on a log,
The dog was sick.
After my toy it did lick,
I was so very sad,
Because the dog was so bad,
So my parents bought me a new toy,
They didn't want to see a sad boy,
So, now I keep it away,
When there's a dog in my way.

Azi Kramer

Clouds

C louds come and clouds go, always maintaining a steady flow.

L ike dreams floating in the sky, they light up my mind as I walk by.

O ut on the ocean, up above the hills, perfection can never be lost with such skills.

U nder the mountain, resting on trees, clouds follow you just like bees.

D esert islands, just round the bend, clouds visit, still old friends.

S urrounding a city, weaving around houses, clouds are just big people, wearing white blouses.

Gaïa Renverse Harris (11)

In The City Of Despair

Clouds of integrity lurking longingly above me,
Paths of sorrow leading you to misery,
Treacherous towns of only ugliness, woe
and anger,
Bridges of friendship that take you on voyages to
dead ends of unfaithful, unsafe situations,
Factories of freedom in never-ending daydreams,
Lamposts of love dead in devastation,
Windows of agony pushed out by bitterness,
And railings of reality stopping any spot of joy
from arriving at the palace of nightmares.

Elise Murray (10)

The Twenty-Fourth Night

Comes down the chimney
Ho-ing away
Dashing with reindeer in his sleigh
Eating the pies
Leaving the crumbs
Downing the milk
Bringing the gifts for all the young ones
The day has arrived and everyone is merry
They all gather around and cheer with a sherry
Winter alas with all the snow
Who doesn't like it, I don't know
Christmas is coming tomorrow
And excitement is here
But still, a dark turn will appear on Christmas.

Archer Gray (10)

Writing A Poem

People say writing is hard,
They would be right,
It's tough enough to write a birthday card,
But it can also be amazing to write under the light,
The opportunities are endless, you can have so much fun,
Well, as long as you have a good time,
And if you really like it, you will feel like you are never done,
You will never give up and feel sublime,
So in conclusion, writing is not hard,
Well, that's only if you really care for what you are writing, including a birthday card.

Edmund de Silva (12)

The Seaside

The sand, as fine as salt.
The water, as calm as a koala.
The palm trees swaying in the wind.
Boats, kayaks, catamarans and paddleboards
abandoned, left in a derelict state, washed up
on the beach.
Ice cream trucks and hot dog stands, awaiting
customers.
Twigs, rocks, leaves and bugs hide under the sand,
searching for their next victim.
Children play in the bay, climbing over the waves,
so come and spend a day away.
This is the way of the seaside.

Isaac Coulibaly (12)

Space Dream

My dream is to name a star
While playing the guitar.
My dream is to gaze through a telescope,
To know how space can cope
With all the shiny, dazzling stars
And what secret lives lie beyond.
My dream is to watch a shooting star
As it glides through the night sky afar.
But my real dream is to become an astronaut.
My dream is to go to the moon
To explore the galaxy and soon
My dream is to see the Milky Way,
Far, far beyond and away.

Noor Elkider (9)

The Train To France

A train from St Pancras we took
Out of the window, I looked
A castle I saw up the hill
That gave me an almighty thrill

The next thing I saw was a tree
With birds flying around it all free
We go to our hotel and have a crepe
My sister stopped by to stroke a pet

Sadly in three days, we would have to come back
But then we would be carrying an extra sack
When we came back it was so warm
But as I stepped into my house I sadly stepped
on a thorn.

Nico Luehrmann (9)

Magic

There is magic everywhere you see,
Over the rooftops and in the sea,
Some make you chuckle and pop,
And maybe they make you hop,
Look carefully at the leaves on the trees,
Eating cake and dancing with the breeze,
Listen carefully to the malicious witch's cackle,
Occasionally it makes you rattle,
Oh, how prepossessing it looks,
Fantastic flowers are transforming into hooks,
There is magic everywhere you see,
Over the rooftops and in you and me!

Liliana Christine Valentina Rob (11)

Giraffes

Looming over you like a majestic, loyal tree
Listening carefully to its trustworthy friends
Its neck reaches over you like a twisted,
turning mountain
Glorious tongue, as purple as a freshly
picked grape.
Leaves getting squashed in their refreshed
mouths; grinding
Legs as tall as thin stilts, reaching up toward
the dappled, rising sun.
Giraffes' horns (ossicones) swaying gently atop
its high, useful head.

Leila Clifford (9)

Anxiety

Yeah, I'm fine if 'F' is for
Feeling overwhelmed and I
Is for I'm not alright, yeah
I'm fine if 'N' is for not
Being able to sleep, 'E' for
Every night! Yeah, I'm fine,
Fine-ally feeling the
Pressure of keeping my
Feelings inside, yeah, I'm
Fine, well, maybe I'm not
And I just need to tell
Someone I'm not alright.

Kylan Hand (11)

Friendships

They are helpful and kind
They take you on journeys that are hard to find
They cheer you up when you're feeling down
By playing a board game and acting like a
silly clown
You'll play on your Nintendo Switch
Or kick a ball on a football pitch
You'll eat some popcorn and burgers
And watch Arsenal play Tottenham Hotspurs
You may fall out, but that is fine
As you will make up in a very short time.

Dilan Tanna (9)

Leopards

L eaping tree to tree in the sun, loving life

E njoying the beautiful, sunny, savannah

O n the lookout for prey, crouching in the long, high grass

P acing through the lush, green trees

A s graceful as a ballerina

R eady to play (but not on the monkey bars)

D ancing in the daylight, their fur ruffling in the warm breeze

S trike!

Nancy Clifford (9)

Garden Things

A slippery slimy slug,
A creepy crawly bug.
Plodding in the sun,
Let's have some fun!

A silky white web,
Comes down in Feb.
Dewdrops on the silk thread,
Makes the web a shiny tread.

Water falls on the trails,
Made by snails.
They come out in the night,
With the moonlight.
They go back inside,
When the sun is shining bright.

Vanya Mehta (8)

Glory

The ball is in the player's hands
Big roar from the stands
The ball is flying through the air
All they can do is stop and stare
The ball's in the net without a sound
In amazement, he falls to the ground
One more minute the team's almost won
5, 4, 3, 2, 1...
The team hold the trophy high in the sky
On the leaderboard, the team is really high.

Thomas Osguthorpe

The Fox Hole

Foxes play in the night
They scuttle away in fright
When all alone
They come out to play
When their mum barks
They go back in the dark
The foxes snuggle into their mother.

In the dark hole the foxes' fur bristles on their skin
Till their mum licks it soft again
The vixen's eyes gleam with protection
When all clear she goes out for prey
Jumps and scuttles
Her cubs follow her home barking.

Emily Hilton-Dennis (7)

Night Owl

When you see a feather at night,
You'll know it's an owl.
When you see a shine of bright,
You'll know it's an owl's sight.

Wisping through the trees,
You might feel a little breeze,
A brush against your arm
Sends a shiver up your arm.
When the sun comes up
It's time to rise, but owls are
Only made for night eyes.

Shreya Anna Morgan (10) & Calicee

Who's Misery?

Misery grabs your nerves
When you're into the gloom
Forevermore, you will suffer
He speaks quietly in the room.

Not wanting to show himself
Staring at you, speechless
If I dare you to go near him
You'll find yourself gnashed into pieces.

Misery never fades away
Whether you're hanging from a cliff
Or a spider biting every toe
It's endlessly quite stiff.

Amelia Poon (8)

Stitch

S o smart with a heart of gold

T iny and adorable with a baby blue colour

I n Hawaii, he lives with his best friend, Lilo

T remendous adventures with Jumba and Pleakley

C ute and cuddly, even though he comes from another world

H e was taught that 'Ohana' means family and family means nobody gets left behind and forgotten.

Zahra Ben-Saïd (8)

Sea And Sand

Waves make each grain dance,
Leaving remnants of glass.
Particles so tiny,
Each molecule so shiny.

Each fragment full of cheers,
Laughter, memories and tears.
The sun beats down, the waves crash in,
And, in the sand, our footprints spin.

The tide begins to recede,
And the sand calls out in need.
Leaving it to bake by day and chill at night,
Until the sea and sand reunite.

Krish Daswani (8)

The Bird Filled With Sorrow

The bird filled with sorrow
Sitting on a branch
Sad
Lonely
Worried
Mad
All alone
Foxes eating birdie bone
No hope or bird in the distance
Gone inside
Heart lost
Almost winter
Birdie froze from the frost
Gone away
No hope today
Just lost and sad and maybe mad
Just gone and dead in this instance.

Jasmine Darrell Pearse (9)

Life Without Plastic

Life without plastic,
Just wouldn't it be fantastic?

Colourful coral swaying from side to side,
Curious clownfish playing in low tide.

Seeing turtles, whales and jellyfish too,
Swimming without any worries, if only that
were true.

If our oceans finally became clean,
This poem would no longer be a dream.

Aariya Tirahan (9)

A Life Of Nature

While walking on the track
I have my backpack with me.
While strolling on a sunny day
I realise that it is the first of May.
With my trainers on the ground,
I can feel the shifting breeze.
When a leaf landed on my cheek
It vanished out of nowhere.
A little robin flew over me
When I was about to run to it.
The trees began to shake
Before I was taken back to my place.

Kabiven Vivekanantharajah (11)

My Pet Unicorn

When I walked into IKEA,
I had a bright idea,
To ride a unicorn,
Right until dawn,
Her mane would glow,
Like a beautiful rainbow,
She would sit on a cloud,
And neigh very loud,
I called her Sunshine,
Did you know she was nine?
Her nickname was Sunny,
Oh, she was funny,
I would laugh and laugh and laugh.

Alaina Holland (9)

Puppies Are The Best

Haiku poetry

Fluffy, cuddly, cute
Energetic waggy tails
Puppies are so sweet.

Licky, friendly, fun
Chasing balls is what they love
Always so happy.

Floppy ears, big eyes
Will do anything for treats
They are full of charm.

Playful, cheeky friends
Love joining in a fun game
Chasing their own tails.

Loyal, loving pets
Happily snoozing all day
Puppies are the best.

Oliver Penderis (9)

Family

F antastic parents (also step-parents)

A wesome sibling (but sometimes annoying)

M arvellous cousins (or mischievous friends)

I ncredible aunts and uncles (if you want a gift, you know who to ask)

L oving grandparents (also very much adventurous)

Y ou're a part of this family (surely the most important one).

Lucas Filippini (11)

The Magic Spot

A long majestic trail
I see a line that all shall hail
A fly dancing in front of me
A fly that only I can see
Some bark that I can feel
Some bark that cannot be a meal
Birds singing my name
But it is not me with all the fame
Taste is what I can't place
But maybe if I keep the pace
I can smell the beautiful outside
Like two worlds can collide.

Daniel Holmes (9)

Be Happy

When I am happy...
The world becomes very big.
The people become very nice.
The food becomes very tasty.
My eyes become very big and they start
to glow with happiness.
My face becomes very pretty with a big
cheerful smile.
And I become a very friendly person.
That's why it is important to be happy.

Maria Qasir (7)

Swimming

S pearfishing for the win

W et, wavy water knocks me out of control

I dive with power into the blue

M otivation for the gold medal

M ove your arms, pulling dumbbells through the water

I fight with adrenaline

N ever give up

G liding, streamline to reach the wall.

Jacob Mellors (10)

Fear

Fear is as dark as space
Fear is like you're in the wrong place.

Fear is your heart beating at light speed,
Fear is your mind saying, *retreat!*

Fear is hands grabbing you,
Fear is getting stuck in the loo.

Fear is getting late for school
Fear is jumping into the pool.

Fear is voices in your head.
Fear is the scary book you read.

Aaron Bijoy (8)

Mermaid

Under the sea you are free,
Singing and flapping your scaly tail,
To the whispers of the sea within,
Seeing your beauty as you emerge from the sea.
You are immortal beneath the surface,
Trembling in your soft and snowy nest,
Drooling in your ocean
Of lonely tears, as wave upon wave
Washes upon you, as your beauty is gazed upon.

Precious Adeyomoye (10)

Happiness

I am candyfloss at a funfair
A hot summer's day after endless rain
The ticket to feeling good
Everyone likes me
Everyone likes me
Licking lollies in the sunshine
Relaxing on the rug
But you can't always be happy
That's just too hard
Always remember that
It will come.

Maya Bordia (9)

Prowling Tiger

Auburn-gold summer breeze
Amber gaze like two orange suns
A sheen of sunlit river he wears
Glints like the faded teeth he bears

Dark slits of starry night
Adorn him
He burns light
Like a falling star.

He pads across his silent
Hidden kingdom
Whispers of breath escape from his might -
Nothing may stain his beauty bright.

Jaya Knox (11)

Live!

Flowers, oh flowers,
Watch the sunflowers turn to the sun,
And the dog roses dance in the wind.

Trees, oh trees,
The oak sprouts, the blossom flowers and fruits.

Grasses, oh grasses,
Let the cornflower scatter its seeds,
And the daisy be happy
And let everything live!

Thea Smith (7)

Bloom Time

5am the sun rises,
slowly climbing high.
Red, pink and yellow,
warming up the sky.

12pm petals spreading,
falling open wide.
Purple, yellow and red,
swaying side to side.

9pm the sun sets,
quickly falling low.
Purple, red and orange,
covers land below.

Ruby Nelson (7)

Science

Science is fun with lots of experiments,
Let's make a hypothesis,
So grab your paper and pen.
So many options of things to investigate,
Let's make a potion, whizz, fizz and bang.
Who knows what will happen,
Maybe an explosion.
Let's make some crazy,
The fun never ends.

Sienna Jefferson (8)

My Mum

M y mummy and me!

O n this day, I just want to say, "I love you."

T he love is in both our hearts.

H ere we are together, where it's love, care, it's 100 per cent.

E very day our love is always the same, our hearts,

R eady for care and love.

Maya Harding (7)

Malala

One foot forward, one foot back
Running scared and fighting back
Seeing problems and jumping in
Stand for education for everyone
Shot in the head and bounced back
Secret name on the Internet
Nobel Peace Prize at 17
Grew up willing to go to school
Changing the world right now.

Tess Bas (9)

Poetry

P oetry is a kind of book, but

O nly with a special rule, from

E asy poems to hard, it must follow

T hat rule... It must

R hyme or go acrostic or maybe it's a haiku

Y ou probably saw that this is an acrostic poem,
so actually it's very easy.

Hanna Shum (8)

Ice Cream

The tasty strawberry kind
Is what you may find.

A minty choc-chip taste,
But do not waste,
That taste like toothpaste.

A vanilla touch
Or maybe with a hint of fudge.

Also, a kind of rum and raisin,
When you eat it, you should be praising.

There is a caramel one,
When you eat it, it is so fun.

Sophia Dunne (9)

Science

People think physics is for nerds
But it's as easy as words
Practise makes perfect
The answer just clicked

Biology is more than a body
It's everything and everybody
That lives on Earth
And can give birth
It can be a seed or an animal.

Elizabeth Hurley (11)

Space

S pace is amazing, sacred, beautiful and outstanding.

P lanets swirling around the fire-red sun.

A stronauts exploring the amazing rock moon.

C old Neptune is the second furthest away from the sun.

E verything in space is never-ending.

Aletheia Ng (8)

The Forest

F ull of trees and creatures,
O dious smell not so far,
R adiant flowers shine,
E piphytes all around waiting to trap their prey,
S piders spinning their webs in elegant designs,
T all dark trees shadow nature's beauty.

Safa Bhatti (10)

The Willow

Its long, slender branches towered above me,
Reaching up to the soft, fluffy clouds.

Intertwining.

As the dappled light fell around me in shades of
Emerald green.

Forever in an embrace.

I was at peace with the world.

Ariella Sheridan (10)

What Football Stadium Am I?

I can hold 53,400 fans
Construction started in 2000
I am the 6th largest football stadium in England
I am on the east side of Manchester
My rival is the southwest side
I am four miles away from my rival club
Which stadium am I?

Answer: Etihad Stadium.

Brook Laycock (10)

We Need To Save Our World

We need to save our planet
Slowly, slowly, our world fades away,
Slowly, slowly, our world is dying.
While we sit and do nothing,
Global warming is rising.
All that plastic in the sea,
It really is a shame.
So, I plea,
Make our world great again
Or else, it will wane.

Rishika Raushan (10)

Birthday

B est day ever
I ncredible dancing
R oaring cheers
T ime to eat as much as you want
H oarse throats after singing 'Happy Birthday'
D elightful friends and family
A mazing cakes
Y our favourite time of year.

Olutowo Omotoso

Chester Zoo

C heetahs

H ippopotamus

E lephants

S nakes

T igers

E mu

R hinoceros

Z ebras

O rangutans

O tters

This is why Chester Zoo is the best.

Aycha Ben-Saïd (7)

Sunflowers

It starts as a simple seed
So small yet so vivid

It grows and grows
Until it can no more

And with its vibrant petals
And its radiant stem

It fades away each autumn
Like the moon does each awesome day.

Meerab Shahab

Jungle Animals

The beautiful butterfly flutters through the air
as a leaping lion descends on its prey.
A fantastic flamingo plays games with some
leaping feisty frogs
While some jungle animals hear a cackle from
swinging magic monkeys throughout the day.

Darcey Molloy (9)

Spring

S inging birds from the trees
P erfect flowers shooting up
R inging bluebells from the ground
I n the burrows, new bunnies are made
N ice sunshine and rain is here
G lorious time of the year.

Smriti Phani (7)

A Poem

The
Best way to
Write a poem is to
Close your eyes then think
Really hard, then concentrate and
Once you get ideas write them down quickly.
Plan it down slowly and before you know it
You've made...
A poem!

Victory Chiamaka

You Can Fly

You can fly my dear!
There's nothing to fear.

Just focus
And hocus pocus!

You can fly my dear!
Don't waste your tears.

You can fly!
Just give it a try.

You can fly my dear!

Siddhi Garg (11)

Trio Of Moths

Elephant Hawk-moth
Honeysuckle camouflaged
Rose and green velvet

A Pale Tussock moth
Like a little furry bat
In a hawthorn tree

A Privet Hawk moth
Fluttering in the cold air
Biggest of its kind.

William Dewhurst (10)

My Spring Poem

Birds sing
Time for spring
Flowers sprout
Butterflies are out.

Say bye to the snow
And hey to the sun
Step outside and let's have fun!

Spring is here
Time to cheer
The sun is near.

Connie Oldham (8)

Environment Day

Plants are good for the environment.
Plant a seed in a pot.
Water it.
Let it grow a shoot and a root.
This is called germination.
Plants are healthy.
Plastic is bad, especially littering.
Do not use plastic!

Omswaroop Kotti (7)

Flowers

Like in some wood,
Like sea is bright,
Glowing in the light,
In the sky,
I want to ask why.
But when you walk away
I think you should stay
So you can discover
What is inside the flower
And what a surprise!
When you open your eyes.

Mrinal Sumesh (7)

Dinosaur

D inosaurs...
I ncredibly sharp teeth
N oisy roars
O cean explorers
S cary stomps
A s tall as a tree
U nexpectedly some are fast
R azor-sharp claws.

Frankie Lee Hook (7)

Dog

A kennings poem

Powerful barker
Bone sucker
Astonishing runner
Adorable looker
Detective sniffer
Cat chaser
Meat devourer
Lazy sleeper
Strong worker
Incredible swimmer
Memory saver.

Sai Nandhan Reddy Narravula (8)

Winter

W arm hot chocolate
I cicles hanging from the roofs
N ever warm, unless by a toasty fire
T asty Christmas dinner
E nraging snowball fights
R ivers frozen over.

Megan Griffiths (8)

Chicken Nugget Limerick

Baking in the oven, hot, crispy and golden,
To the Chicken Nugget gods I am beholden,
Mouth-watering, definitely delicious,
Plate piled high, looking ambitious,
Finally, McNuggets, Amen.

Sebastian Forman (8)

What Am I?

I own lovely kids and teachers,
I'm always here for learners.
I'm full of students,
Don't forget the teachers.
I begin with an A.
What am I?

Sidney Hurst-Keast

My Favourite Animal ~ A Riddle Poem

Yellow and black with spots
Razor-sharp teeth
Fastest animal on land
Also, very lazy mostly?
Antelope, gazelle and impalas
I eat them all
I live in Africa only

What am I?

Sebastian Hodges (9)

A Poem About Summer

S wimming in the sea
U nder the sun
M eeting my friends
M aking sandcastles
E verybody is happy
R unning on the beach.

Christian Uche Nwachukwu (7)

Secrets

Secrets are as black as death.
As dim as mess.
As distrustful as the mind.
Horrible things secrets are.
They burn a hole in your heart.

Bethany Lee (11)

Seagull

A haiku

Swooping through the sky
Stealthily stealing ice creams
Surreptitiously.

Douglas Maconochie

Britain

A haiku

King Charles, our ruler
Union Jack on the flag
London Eye, spinning.

Gabriel Orr (9)

Daisies

A haiku

The tiny daisies
Open petals under sun
Rain... Shy petals close.

Sky Kwok (9)

YOUNG WRITERS INFORMATION

We hope you have enjoyed reading this book – and that you will continue to in the coming years.

If you're the parent or family member of an enthusiastic poet or story writer, do visit our website **www.youngwriters.co.uk/subscribe** and sign up to receive news, competitions, writing challenges and tips, activities and much, much more! There's lots to keep budding writers motivated!

If you would like to order further copies of this book, or any of our other titles, then please give us a call or order via your online account.

Young Writers
Remus House
Coltsfoot Drive
Peterborough
PE2 9BF
(01733) 890066
info@youngwriters.co.uk

YoungWritersUK
YoungWritersCW **youngwriterscw**

Scan me to watch the Poetry Towers video!